W9-CKH-486

For Mam and Dad,
remembering other travels, through
storm and flood, by post office van.

Copyright © 1990 by Peter Haswell
First American Edition 1990 published by Orchard Books

All rights reserved. No part of this book may be reproduced or
transmitted in any form or by any means, electronic or mechanical,
including photocopying, recording or by any information storage or
retrieval system, without permission in writing from the Publisher.

Orchard Books
A division of Franklin Watts, Inc.
387 Park Avenue South
New York, NY 10016

First published in Great Britain by Walker Books Ltd., London

Printed by South China Printing Co., Hong Kong (1988) Limited

10 9 8 7 6 5 4 3 2 1

The text of this book is set in 20 pt. Veronan Light 2

Library of Congress Cataloging-in-Publication Data
Haswell, Peter
Pog climbs Mount Everest/written and illustrated by Peter Haswell – 1st American ed.
p. c.m.
"Originally published by Walker Books Ltd."
Summary: Getting a cup of tea inspires Pog to climb Mount Everest.
ISBN 0-531-05873-5. – ISBN 0-531-08473-6 (lib. bdg.)
[1. Pigs – Fiction. 2. Humorous stories.] I. Title.
PZ7.H2815Pp 1990   89-26530
[E] – dc20   CIP
                              AC

POG
climbs
Mount Everest

Written and illustrated by

PETER HASWELL

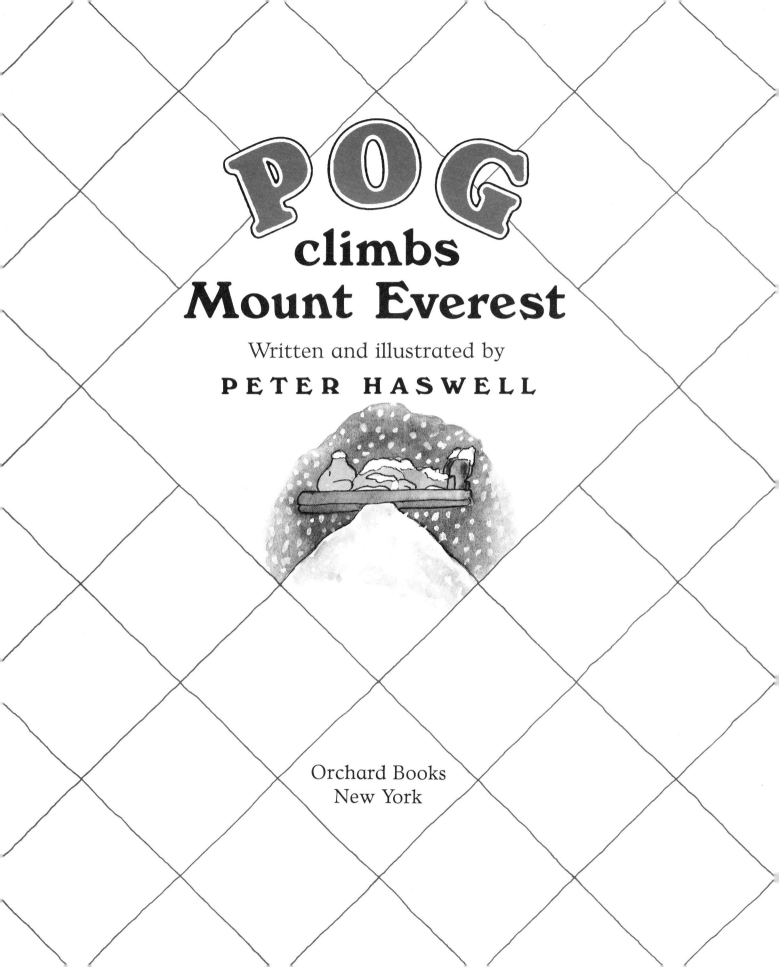

Orchard Books
New York

Pog wanted a cup of tea.

His cup was on the top shelf

of the dresser.

Pog climbed

on a chair and

got it down.

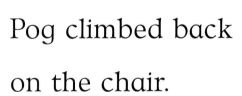

The teapot was on top of the dresser.

Pog climbed back
on the chair.

But this time he couldn't reach.

Pog put some books on the chair
and climbed up again.
Now he could reach.

But because his hands were full,

he couldn't climb down.

Pog put the teapot back.

Now he could climb down, but he still
did not have the teapot.

"Never mind," said Pog. "I enjoyed the climb
so much I think I'll climb Mount Everest now.
And I'll have some tea when I get back."

Pog set out for Mount Everest.

"The problem is," said Pog, "I don't know the way to Mount Everest. I'd better ask."

Pog asked a street light.

It didn't answer.

Pog asked a garbage pail.

It didn't answer.

Pog asked a cardboard box. It didn't answer.

"Hmm," said Pog. "This is not going to be easy.

Nobody knows the way to Mount Everest."

Pog came to a corner. He stopped.

"If I go around this corner," he said,

"I might never find my way back."

Pog pondered.

"On the other hand," said Pog,

"if I don't go around this corner,

I might never find Mount Everest."

Pog pondered again.

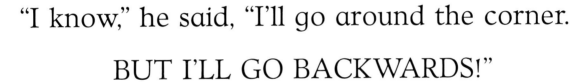

"I know," he said, "I'll go around the corner.

BUT I'LL GO BACKWARDS!"

"That way I'll be able to see which way I've come."

Pog walked.

He walked along a street.

He walked through a door.

Pog began
to climb.
"I seem to be
climbing up,"
said Pog.
"Mount Everest
is up."

"Yippee!
I've climbed
Mount
Everest."

Pog walked into a room.

"Good heavens," he said, "I didn't know

Mount Everest was a room!"

Suddenly a man sat up in bed.

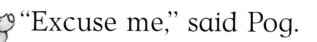

"Excuse me," said Pog.

"Is this Mount Everest?"

"Mount Everest?" said the man. "Certainly not!

Mount Everest is .... that-a-way."

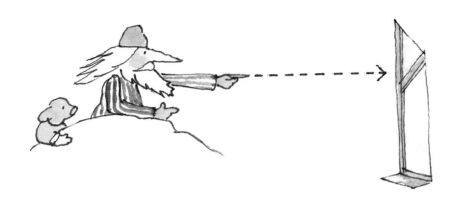

Pog went that-a-way.

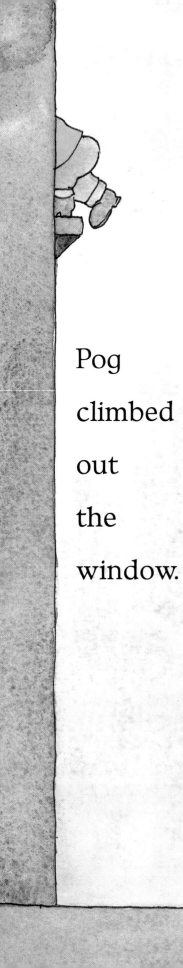

Pog climbed out the window.

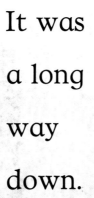

It was a long way down.

Pog jumped.

The man looked out the window.

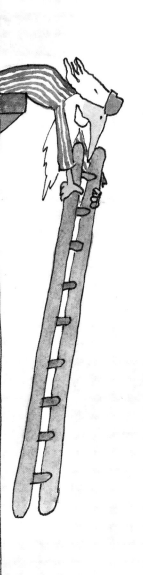

"Just a
minute,"
shouted
the man.
"I've got
a ladder."

"Isn't it a
bit late
for a
ladder?"
asked Pog.

"Not at
all,"
said the
man.
"You can
use it to
climb
Mount
Everest."

Pog walked to Mount Everest.

He walked for four years.

29,029 feet

Pog arrived at Mount Everest.

Pog leaned the ladder

against Mount Everest.

He climbed the ladder.

"Oh dear," said Pog.

"It doesn't reach."

"On the other hand,

it does reach the ground."

"Maybe it's a ladder for going down

instead of for going up."

"I know. I'll carry the ladder up Mount Everest

and use it for climbing down."

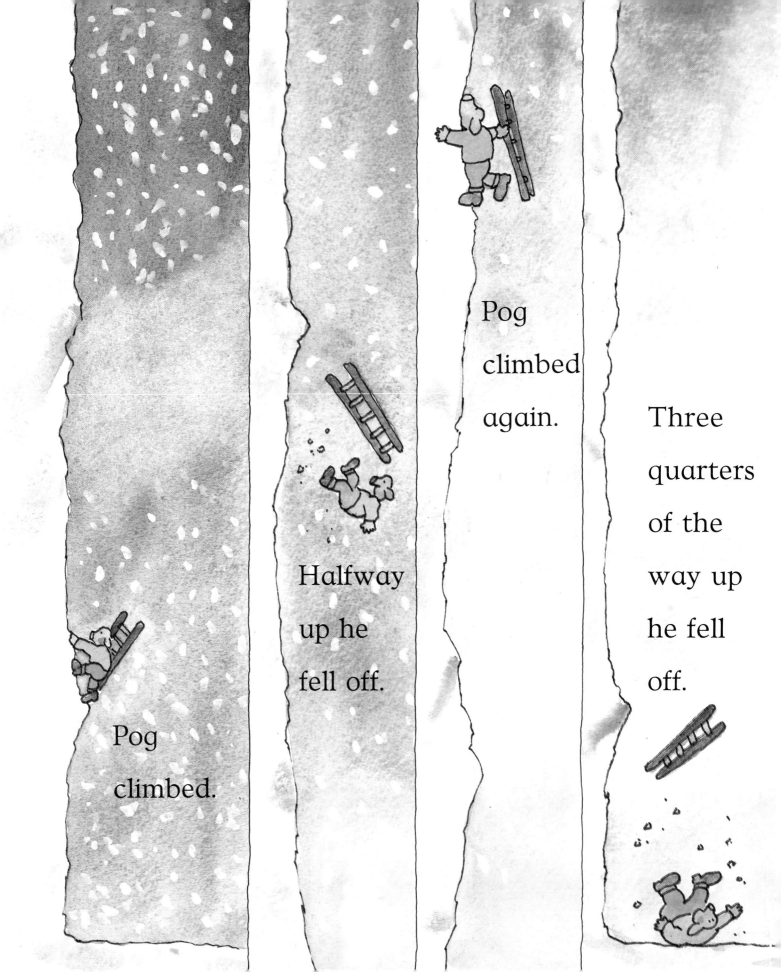

Pog climbed.

Halfway up he fell off.

Pog climbed again.

Three quarters of the way up he fell off.

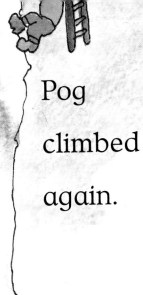

Pog

climbed

again.

Pog reached the summit. "Whew!"

said Pog. "Not only have I climbed

Mount Everest, I've climbed it

TWO AND A QUARTER TIMES!"

Then Pog had an idea.

Pog climbed down Mount Everest

and ran home.

Pog boiled some water.
He stood the ladder
against the dresser.

Then he climbed up with the ,

the , the , his , and a 🥄.

Pog made tea.

Pog drank his cup of tea.

"It was a nice cup of tea,"
said Pog. "But I think it
will be my last for a while...."

"Aaaaaaaaaargh!"

"Yoo hoo.

May we have some

tea?"